Because You're Mine

Nancy Tillman

FEIWEL AND FRIENDS

NEW YORK

The moment that you came along
my heart grew mighty, fierce and strong,
and everything just fell from view.
All that I could see was you.

The world may circle 'round your head
and wish that you were its instead,

but that can never, ever be . . .

because you belong to me.

The clouds can blow.
The rain can fall.
The snow can come.
The wind can call.

But they'll just
have to wait
in line . . .

Because you're mine.

Because you're mine.

There's nothing that the world can do
to get ahead of my love for you.

Nothing you can do or say
can ever take my love away.

Happy, silly, cross, or wild,
you are my amazing child.

Every day I love you more
than all the days that came before.

So if some twisty turny day
you see that you have lost your way,
no matter what I need to do,
I will find my way to you.

I'll jump every puddle
and row every pond . . .

I'll cross every meadow
and mountain beyond—

until you're snuggled
safe and fine.

Because you're mine. Because you're mine.

I'll tell you a secret that you never knew.
All of my life I've been waiting for you.

Me and you. You and me.
We were always meant to be.

Although I know you'll grow one day
and I will watch you sail away,
this mighty heart that loves you so
will go wherever winds can blow.

And when they blow you back to me,
what a joy that day will be!

For any time and any place
I see your sunny, funny face,
my heart will cheer,
my eyes will shine—

Because you're mine. Because you're mine.

The reverse is just as true—I also belong to *you*.

To my perfect grandson, Wes Carlucci.
Our love story is just beginning.

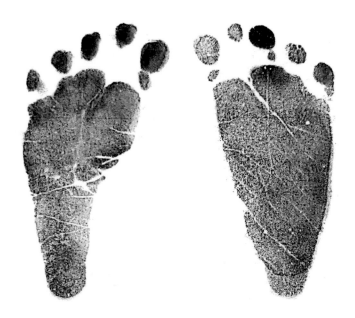

A FEIWEL AND FRIENDS BOOK
An imprint of Macmillan Publishing Group, LLC
120 Broadway, New York, NY 10271

Our books may be purchased in bulk for promotional, educational, or business use. Please contact your local bookseller or the Macmillan Corporate and Premium Sales Department at (800) 221-7945 ext. 5442 or by email at MacmillanSpecialMarkets@macmillan.com.

Library of Congress Cataloging-in-Publication Data is available.

ISBN 978-1-250-25613-3 (hardcover)

Feiwel and Friends logo designed by Filomena Tuosto

First edition, 2020
The artwork was created digitally using a variety of software painting programs on a Wacom tablet. Layers of illustrative elements are first individually created, then merged to form a composite. At this point, texture and mixed media (primarily chalk, watercolor, and pencil) are applied to complete each illustration.

1 3 5 7 9 10 8 6 4 2

mackids.com

You are loved.